"We are going to Bergen, and there we will take a steamship to New York," Papa said firmly. "We are not turning back."

I felt as though I were falling down into the dark water with the white jellyfish and the chunks of ice. It was a frightening feeling, and I took two quick steps away from the railing. What if America didn't want us, after all? What if nobody in America spoke Norwegian? What if I never had another friend like Holger? The more I thought about it, the more frightened I became. But I could not let anyone know that. Wasn't I Lili the Brave?

CHILDREN OF AMERICA

Lili
the Brave

by Jennifer Armstrong
illustrated by Uldis Klavins

A STEPPING STONE BOOK
Random House 🏠 New York

http://www.randomhouse.com/

Library of Congress Cataloging-in-Publication Data
Armstrong, Jennifer
Lili the brave / by Jennifer Armstrong ; illustrated by Uldis Klavins.
p. cm. — (Children of America)
"A stepping stone book."
SUMMARY: A spirited young girl does not want to leave her home in Norway
to go to live in Minnesota, but aboard ship on the way to America, she proves
why she is called "Lili the Brave."
ISBN 0-679-87286-8 (pbk.) — ISBN 0-679-97286-2 (lib. bdg.)
[1. Emigration and immigration—Fiction.   2. Norwegian Americans—Fiction.
3. Brothers and sisters—Fiction.   4. Courage—Fiction.]
I. Klavins, Uldis, ill.   II. Title.   III. Series.
PZ7.A73367Lh   1997   [Fic]—dc21   97-11219

Contents

CHAPTER 1

The Man from America

It was a rainy spring day when Mr. Rolvang came to our town. I was making a straw braid for baby Asa while we all waited outside our houses. Most of the people in Vinhaven didn't even mind the wet. They were curious to see the man from America.

Suddenly, the people in the street began chattering and calling out to one another. They were louder than the sea gulls when the fishing boats come in. The butcher's dog began to bark.

"Here he comes—up the hill!"

"It's Mr. Rolvang, who left Norway so long ago!"

"He went to America and grew fat on meat and cakes!" Mrs. Helm said to me. "You can see, Lili, what a great man he is."

"I can't see anything but Mr. Olafsen's back," I grumbled.

My mama tugged my hair. "Mind your manners, Lili. And don't speak to Mr. Rolvang unless he speaks to you first."

"I won't speak to him at all," I said.

I peeked around the legs and skirts of the Vinhaven folks. The cobblestones under their seaboots and wooden clogs were shiny wet. Up the hill from the harbor walked a tall, fat man with a bushy beard. He wore a fancy coat.

People called to one another in loud whispers.

"Mr. Rolvang is speaking with Pastor Holmquist now!"

"He's shaking hands with Squinty Larsen the Tailor!"

"He is talking about the state called Minnesota."

"The railroad companies have sent him to us! They want us in America!"

"We won't have to scrimp and save here in poor Norway anymore!"

The fat man in the fancy coat stood on the church steps.

"Good people of Vinhaven!" Rolvang boomed in a loud walrus voice. "I left Norway fifteen years ago with nothing in my pockets. But now I am a rich man! In America, anyone who works hard can be a success."

I said "Bosh" in a low voice and bent my

head over my straw braid. I decided not to believe a word he said.

My little brother, Haakon, was so amazed by Rolvang he forgot to close his mouth. I pushed Haakon's chin up for him.

"You'll catch flies," I whispered.

"In America, land is cheap!" Rolvang said.

"Bosh," I muttered again. Land was only for the rich. Everyone in Norway knew that.

"And the railroad company will help pay for your passage! It is only forty American dollars from Norway to Minnesota. Ship and train fare."

Behind me, Papa let out a whistle. "Heaven above!"

"You see, all his clothes are store-bought!" Mama said to Mrs. Helm.

"Mr. Rolvang is a smart man," Mrs. Helm

said, nodding wisely. "Your husband should listen to him, Mrs. Alesund."

My straw braid suddenly came all unbraided. I looked up at Papa and Mama. "It's all bosh," I warned them. "Don't follow his advice."

"Minnesota is the heavenly land of your dreams!" Rolvang boomed.

I glared at him. The heavenly land of my dreams was Norway. At the center of heaven was our beautiful town on the edge of the sea. We had everything we could want in Vinhaven. We had fish and whales from the ocean. We had cloud-berries and reindeer from the land. We had sunshine on summer nights. And in the long, dark winter, we had the beautiful northern lights in the night sky. They waved like flags made of stars. Mama said they made her think of angels dancing.

"We have talked about it, Mrs. Helm," Mama said to our neighbor. She put baby Asa on her other shoulder. "We have talked late many nights."

Mrs. Helm smiled down at me. Her eyes disappeared in her wrinkles. "Lili, isn't Mr. Rolvang a fine man to invite you to Minnesota?"

I folded my arms. I stuck my chin in the air. "Vinhaven is our home. I don't listen to a fat walrus man in store-bought clothes." I spoke in a loud and bold voice.

"Lili!" Mama gasped.

There was a hush. The crowd parted around us, and Rolvang stood before me. Up close, he was much, much bigger than I thought. He was like a huge shaggy bear.

"So, this is a brave girl who knows her

mind!" the big man from America boomed.

Papa shoved me behind Mama. "Please excuse her manners, sir."

"Hmmph!" Rolvang stepped to one side so he could still stare at me with his sharp eyes. I stood up even straighter. I was too brave to let him frighten me. The crowd was silent. Everyone watched.

Someone nearby whispered, "He is speaking with the Alesund family!"

"America is good to people with spirit," the man from America announced. He made his bushy eyebrows bristle at me. "This is the type of girl Minnesota wants!"

"She's strong," Papa said quickly.

"And smart," Mama added.

"I don't want to go to America!" I yelled. "You look like a walrus!"

Rolvang threw his head back and roared

with laughter. "Come to America, Mr. Alesund," he said to Papa. "Bring your whole
family. Will you come?"

Mama and Papa turned to each other
with shining eyes. They looked as if they
were seeing heaven's holy angels.

"We will come, sir," Papa said.

"We will come, sir," Mama agreed.

Rolvang winked at me.

I knew that meant we were going to America. I would never see the northern lights dancing over Vinhaven again.

CHAPTER 2

The Viking Ship

My friend Holger came to our house in the morning. He cried. Anything could start him crying. He cried when the harbor turned red with whale blood. He cried when the harbor turned red with the setting sun. Mama says he's one of the tender ones.

I never cried. Even the time I got a fish hook stuck in my finger and Papa had to cut it out with a very sharp knife, I did not cry. Because of that, some people in Vinhaven had a special name for me: Lili the Brave.

Holger wiped his eyes. "Lili, stay here in Vinhaven."

"I'm thinking," I told him. I frowned hard at the kitchen floor. "I'm thinking of a plan."

Mama and Papa were sitting in the parlor by the blue and white stove. Rolvang was showing them papers and asking them to sign. Each time a paper rustled, my heart jumped like a herring in a net. Rustle—jump! But I didn't cry. When you are the oldest, you mustn't cry. I couldn't let Asa see me.

I was rocking Asa. Her cradle was carved to look like a Viking ship. A sea monster curled over the top to protect Asa.

Haakon had lain in that cradle. So had I. The fierce sea monster had protected all of us. Our floor was painted blue, and the cradle looked like a little ship sailing across the sea as it rocked.

Sometimes, when Haakon was very tired or very sad or frightened, he would squeeze himself into the cradle. He curled up very small and tucked in his arms and legs. Of course, I was too big even to try! Or to want to.

I heard Mama come to the door behind me. It gave me an idea.

"Last night I had a dream," I told Holger without looking around. "I dreamed my family was in this cradle and that it was taking us to America."

"It's not a very large cradle," Holger pointed out.

I frowned at him. "In my dream it grew until it was the size of a real Viking ship. But then the sea monster came to life. It

12

turned around and picked up Haakon in its mouth and ate him!"

"Lili!" Holger's eyes grew round and watery. "Were you frightened?"

I still did not look back at my mother. But I knew she was listening. "It was terrible."

Holger took a step closer to me. "What does that dream mean?"

"It means bad luck if we go to America!" I shouted. Asa blinked.

At last I turned around. Mama was standing in the doorway. Her arms were crossed in front of her apron. She was shaking her head.

"Too late, little Lili," Mama said. "We are going. And I think you made that dream up right now."

Holger's eyes filled with tears. "But it

might be true! What if you have bad luck when you go to America? What if you are shipwrecked?"

"Oh, tush," Mama said. She picked up Asa, and the cradle-ship went rocking on the blue floor. Mama settled into a chair and began to sing.

> *"I'm ready now for my last trip—*
> *Sing, sailor, oh!*
> *Away to heaven steers my ship—*
> *Sing, sailor, oh!*
> *I'll sail the way I used to do—*
> *Sing, sailor, oh!*
> *Till Paradise comes into view—*
> *Sing, sailor, oh!*
> *What mighty shouts of joy there'll be—*
> *Sing, sailor, oh!*
> *When I come home there from the sea—*
> *Sing, sailor, oh!"*

Holger and I sat staring at the little rocking ship. We heard Papa and Rolvang clapping.

"Well sung, Mrs. Alesund," Rolvang said, walking into the kitchen. He seemed to take up the whole room, even when he sat down. "You're right to call America paradise. It's heaven."

"Are there angels there?" Holger asked.

I tried to kick him, but he was just out of reach.

Rolvang smiled. "Not angels. But let me tell you what Minnesota is like. It is like the ocean. Wide and rolling, and bursting with life. You can see to the ends of the earth in every direction. At night, you feel you are indeed in heaven, because the stars look close enough to touch."

But the northern lights aren't there, I told myself. And America will never be home.

I gave Rolvang a hard, hard look. It was the same look Pastor Holmquist gives Lars Moe, who drinks too much beer.

"Why does the railroad company send you here?" I asked him. "Why do they want us?"

Rolvang put his hands on his knees. "The railroad goes all the way across America now. But America is big and does not have enough people. They want good strong families like yours to be settlers in the empty country. So they send me here to ask you all to come. They want your papa and mama to buy land near the railroad and become settlers. Will you come, Lili?"

Mama put the baby in the Viking-ship cradle. The sea monster curled over Asa's head to protect her.

I said a prayer in my heart. I prayed the monster would protect us all.

CHAPTER 3

Good-Bye!

Parents never listen to advice from their children. That is why one month later I was standing at the rail of Kasper Amundsen's boat. Vinhaven grew smaller and smaller as we sailed away. I kept my eyes on the blue and green house behind the church. It would never be our house again.

Gulls cried over our heads. The steep cliffs stretched up to the sky on both sides of the fjord. A waterfall called Frija's Tears poured down over the rocks. It was cold, sailing along the bottom of the cliffs. It was late June, and a glacier was melting along the top of the cliffs. Chunks of ice broke away from the cliffs and splashed into the fjord.

"Look, Lili," Haakon said in a happy voice. He was leaning over the rail and pointing at the cold black water of the fjord. Little white jellyfish bobbed up and down in the waves. "They look like stars, don't they?"

I sniffed a little bit. "Yes. But Haakon, you should be sad. We are leaving our home. We are leaving our friends."

"I'm not sad," he said. His eyes sparkled and his cheeks were red from the salty air. "We're having an adventure. Mr. Rolvang said maybe we will see buffalo in America."

"I don't *want* to see buffalo!" I shouted.

Captain Amundsen dug his elbow in Papa's side.

"How's this for buffalo?" he said. He lowered his head and humped his shoulders and pawed the deck with his boots.

He looked a little bit frightening, but I did not let it show.

"I only care for reindeer," I said in a grown-up voice.

The adults all laughed.

"Papa, it's not too late," I begged. I looked back once more toward Vinhaven. But we had turned a bend in the narrow fjord. Our town was gone.

"We are going to Bergen, and there we will take a steamship to New York," Papa said firmly. "We are not turning back."

I felt as though I were falling down into the dark water with the white jellyfish and the chunks of ice. It was a frightening feeling, and I took two quick steps away from the railing. What if America didn't want us, after all? What if nobody in America spoke Norwegian? What if I never had another friend like Holger? The more I thought about it, the more frightened I became. But I could not let anyone know that. Wasn't I Lili the Brave?

"It is a good thing you didn't lose all your money from your business," the captain said to Papa.

I turned to look at Papa.

"That's true," Papa said. "I made some bad mistakes. But at least we have enough to get to Minnesota and begin anew."

"It's because of you that we must leave Norway?" I asked Papa.

He cleared his throat. "It is business, Lili.

You wouldn't understand."

"But you said you made bad mistakes!" My voice got higher and higher. "If it weren't for you, we wouldn't have to leave! It's *your* fault!"

"Lili!"

Mama bent down to shush me. But I ran away from them all and stood with my back to the mast. "It's Papa's fault that we must leave our home. I hate him!"

I stared at Papa, and Papa stared at me.

Asa began to cry.

I would never talk to Papa again.

CHAPTER 4

Viking Heroes

Everyone thought I would apologize for my bad behavior. But I didn't. I wasn't sorry. I was angry. I wouldn't speak to Papa.

I didn't speak to him when our boat moved into busy Bergen harbor with its crowd of tall-masted ships. I didn't speak to Papa when Captain Amundsen shouted to the harbormaster through a speaking tube. I didn't speak to Papa when we walked down the bouncing, slippery gangway to the crowded pier.

I didn't speak to Papa when we walked

beneath a crane, and honking geese snowed feathers on us from a crate hanging from a big hook. I didn't speak to him when we checked into a hostel for the night. Even the next morning, when we had our bowls of *rommegrøt* porridge, I would not speak to him. And I didn't speak to him when he left with another papa to buy tickets for the ship.

I went outside the hostel to sit on a bench in the sun. Another girl was there with her grandpa. She had red hair in braids and a round pink face like a berry. She wore reindeer boots and kicked her heels under the bench.

"I'm Lili," I told her.

"I'm Hanne."

"We are going to America," I said. My voice made it sound as if I had said, "We are going down the street."

Hanne looked up at her grandpa and hugged his arm. "We are going, too. I'm excited, aren't you?" she asked me. "It's such an adventure."

I shrugged. "Oh, I suppose so."

"It is the Norwegian way to be hungry for adventure," Hanne's grandpa said. He turned his wrinkled face to the sun. "The great Viking heroes of legend loved adventure. The more dangerous and fearsome, the better!"

Hanne shivered and laughed. "Don't you love scary legends, Lili?"

"I'm not frightened by them," I said.

Hanne looked surprised. "Even when there are horrible trolls and dragons?"

"Oh, trolls don't frighten me a bit," I said. But a shiver suddenly went up my back.

"My goodness," said her grandpa. "You are a brave Viking. Would you be brave enough to go…down?" he asked in a mysterious whisper.

"Down where?" I asked.

"Down—Down—DOWN to NIFELHEIM!" he ended in a shout.

I let out a screech. Hanne's eyes were as wide as a reindeer's. "What is 'Nifelheim'?" she asked.

The old man held up one finger. "Nifelheim is down below in the land of the mists. In Nifelheim the dead dwell forever. And the horrible trolls hammer the rocks with picks and axes. Hammer and pound, pick and chop! Clink! Clank! Hammer and pick in the land of mists! The Viking heroes all had to go to Nifelheim to rescue people captured by trolls."

Another shiver went up my back. At home in Vinhaven, it was easy to be Lili the Brave. But I hadn't even left Norway yet, and I was losing my bravery by the minute.

I took a deep breath. "That's just legend," I said loudly. "Just old folk stories."

"Perhaps," Hanne's grandpa said. "But in our modern times, there are other tests of bravery."

I looked at the ships in the harbor. One of those ships was going to take us over the ocean.

Like the Viking heroes of old, we were going on an adventure. I was certainly glad we wouldn't run into any trolls along the way!

CHAPTER 5

Where Is Haakon?

When Papa returned to the hostel before dinner, he was full of news and instructions. I forgot that I wasn't speaking to him.

"When do we board the ship?" I asked.

"Where will we sleep on the ship?" Haakon wanted to know.

"We'll board after dinner," Papa said. He looked as happy as a puppy with a smelly old fishnet to wrestle. "Our cabin is very, very small, and we can only take our clothes. Everything else must be stored in the cargo hold, down below in the belly of the ship."

"Even the cradle?" Mama asked as she jiggled Asa up and down.

Papa shook his head. "The baby will sleep in the berth with us."

"What is a 'berth'?" Haakon asked.

"On a ship there are special words for many things," Papa said. "A berth is what you call a bed that is built into the cabin wall."

"The beds in Holger's house are like that," Haakon said. "And in Mrs. Helm's house. But they do not call them berths."

"Only on ships do they call them berths," Papa said, laughing.

I did not laugh. I was thinking of the cargo hold, down below.

"What if the cradle is lost?" I asked. I

gave the little Viking ship a pat. I was counting on that fierce sea monster to protect us. "If it is lost on the voyage, what will happen to us?"

"Lili!" Mama laughed. "Don't you mean what will happen to Asa? You don't sleep in the cradle any longer."

I saw Haakon watching me. I didn't want him to think I was frightened.

"Oh, yes," I said. I laughed to show I wasn't at all scared. "I mean what will happen to Asa?"

"If this cradle is lost, we'll get her a new cradle when we reach America," Papa said.

I was shocked at him. "But they would not have a good Norwegian cradle there," I reminded Papa.

He rubbed his hands together. "It doesn't matter. Now let's eat and get on board. We're off to America tonight!"

And then everything became very busy and noisy and confusing. Mama had to repack everything because she thought she had not done a good job the first time. Papa had to give instructions to some sailors from the ship. They would load our feather beds and clocks and crates of household goods and store them in the cargo hold.

Haakon and I were in charge of Asa, and she became worried by all the fuss and began to cry. I had to sing to her and make funny faces to make her smile. I didn't have time to worry about our journey. And then we had to eat our dinner in a rush, and suddenly Mama was tying my hat strings under my chin so tightly that they pinched and then—!

And then we went down to the harbor. At the dock a very large crowd of people waited to board the steamship. The sides of the ship rose up as steep and tall as the sides of a gray cliff. I had a hard lump in my throat when I looked up at the ship. It was difficult to swallow with my hat strings tied so tight.

"Hold on to Haakon's hand," Mama said to me. "Stay close."

Papa had our tickets out. He looked very serious and very excited.

People were shouting and hugging one another and waving good-bye.

"Farewell! God bless you!"

"Good luck in America!"

Haakon squeezed my hand tight.

"Let go for a moment," I whispered. "I have to untie my hat."

My fingers didn't seem to work properly. I was looking up at the enormous ship and trying to untie my hat strings. But the knot would not unravel. I looked up and up and up, and my head tipped back more and more, and my hands fell to my sides. The ship looked as big as a mountain.

A man behind me shouted to a friend and laughed very loud. I turned around to see him. That was when I noticed something very bad.

Haakon was not standing beside me.

I turned this way and that, trying to see through the crowd. My heart was pounding in my ears. Mama and Papa were talking to each other about our cabin, and they did not notice me. I got down on my hands and knees to see between people's legs and around their bags.

"Haakon!" I whispered as loud as I dared. "Haakon!"

I leaned forward to see around a lady's long dress. My eyes were filling with tears. I had lost my little brother!

"Lili? What are you doing on the ground?" Mama's voice turned me to stone.

"Where is Haakon?" Papa asked. "This is no time to be playing games, Lili."

Very slowly, I stood up and faced them. My chin wobbled so hard that I could not speak.

"Where is Haakon?" Mama asked, opening her eyes very wide. *"Where is Haakon?"*

I was too frightened to speak. I opened and shut my mouth like a fish in a net.

Mama looked around wildly. "Haakon!" she cried.

And suddenly there he was, standing in front of Papa.

"When do we go on the ship?" Haakon asked.

I began to cry. At that moment the crowd began to move and someone said, "They are letting us board now!"

CHAPTER 6

Down, Down Below!

It was not until we were finally in our own small cabin that Mama scolded me. She sat me down on the lower berth and told me how much she had counted on me to help her, and how disappointed she was in me. It was chilly in our cabin, and while Mama spoke she wrapped Asa in a wool blanket. I just shivered.

Then Mama and Papa arranged the cabin to their liking. Haakon was hanging upside down from the top berth with his jacket falling over his head. I was wishing I was home in Vinhaven. From far away we heard the faint, lonesome horn of the ship.

Waaaaaah! Waaaaaah!

I climbed into my berth with Haakon and pulled the blankets over my head.

When I opened my eyes again, it was morning. As soon as I was dressed I went up on deck with Haakon. There was no land in sight. Only water. Norway was far behind us.

But the sunshine sparkled brightly on the ocean waves and the salty wind blew in our faces. It was a warm day. We stood behind a lifeboat, where the wind didn't blow so hard. From there we watched people on the deck. Everyone had to walk with their heads ducked against the wind. The smoke from the funnels streamed behind the ship.

Haakon yawned widely, and I yawned right after him.

"Asa cried all night," Haakon complained.

I nodded. "She misses Norway."

"No, I think it is because she didn't sleep in her cradle," Haakon said.

"Lili!" Hanne ran to us and grabbed my hand. "I knew we'd be on the same ship! Isn't it gigantic? I want to explore, but I'm afraid to go alone."

"Lili isn't afraid of anything," Haakon piped up. "At home in Vinhaven people

called her Lili the Brave. We'll go with you."

"Let's go now!" Hanne said, pulling me after her.

There was nothing I could say. Haakon and Hanne both thought I was the bravest one, and so I had to go along. They did not give me any time to dawdle, either. They ran ahead, racing down stairs and passage-ways.

"Come on, Lili!" Haakon's voice echoed around a corner.

I ran after him, just in time to see my brother and Hanne turn another corner.

"Wait!" I shouted. I was panting. "Don't leave me behind!"

What if I lost them? What if we became separated and I got into trouble again? It was a big ship to get lost in!

We kept going down, down, down. One staircase after another. Passageway after passageway. And Haakon and Hanne were always ahead of me, getting farther and farther away.

"Haakon!" I shouted as I ran through a door.

Haakon and Hanne were standing at the top of a staircase, looking down. I stopped beside them. A low, throbbing noise was coming from below, like some giant snoring beast that was having bad dreams.

The air was very warm. In the dim light at the bottom of the stairs, I saw wisps of misty steam. The mist moved slowly around the bottom step, curling and coiling like ghosts.

"You go first," Hanne whispered. She was looking at me.

"Down there?" I asked. I gulped.

"Yes, you first, Lili," Haakon said.

They were both counting on me. I knew I should go down the stairs. But I couldn't make my legs move.

"Down, down, down to Nifelheim," Hanne whispered.

"What?" Haakon asked.

"Nifelheim," Hanne said. She pointed down the stairs where the steam was. "It looks like the land of the mists where the Viking heroes had to go to rescue people from trolls."

"Go on, Lili," Haakon said.

I tried to take a step, but I couldn't. The low, throbbing sound continued, and suddenly there was a loud clank, like a pickax on a rock.

"Do you think there could be trolls down

there?" Hanne asked. She backed away from the staircase.

"Go on, Lili," Haakon said again.

I closed my eyes, took a deep breath, and put one hand on the banister. Then I forced myself to step down one step. Warm, misty air rose into my face. I took another step down, and Haakon and Hanne huddled close behind me.

Step by step by step. That was how we did it, all of us together, with me in the front. Down, down, down. The noise was getting louder and the misty air was getting hotter.

At last, we were at the bottom of the staircase. A passageway led right and left. There was a door at each end.

The door at the right-hand end of the passageway stood slightly open. The noise

was coming from there. Bursts of steam puffed through the narrow gap. Red light glowed around the edge of the door.

"Wh-what is it?" Hanne gasped.

Both Hanne and Haakon were looking at me. Did they think I was going to go look behind that door? Maybe Lili the Brave would. But I was not Lili the Brave any longer. I had turned into Lili the Scared. I would not go that way for all the fish in Norway.

"It's probably nothing," I said. My voice wobbled a little bit. I turned left and headed in the other direction. "Let's explore this way."

Haakon and Hanne followed me. But as we walked away from the mysterious door and the deep, rumbling noise, I had a funny feeling in my back. It was a feeling that we were being watched.

CHAPTER 7

The Door

We tiptoed down the passageway.

Now that the strange light and mist were behind us, I began to feel a bit braver. When we reached the other door, I opened it boldly. I poked my head in, and Hanne and Haakon pushed in behind me.

"Look where we are!" Haakon said. "This must be the cargo hold."

I closed the door, but I could still hear the throbbing noise in the distance. I made sure the door was shut tight. Then I turned to see what the cargo hold looked like.

There was one lamp burning where someone had left it on a hook. It swung slowly back and forth. It made our shadows sway and dance on the door behind us.

By this eerie light we could see boxes and crates and pieces of furniture stacked all around us. There were beds on tables, chairs on dressers, hat stands in baskets. I peeked around a trunk, and my own reflection in a dark mirror made me jump.

"I wonder if my bed is in here!" Hanne said. She squinted to see into the shadows. "It's painted green and yellow with black and white checks on the edge."

"Maybe we could find Asa's cradle," Haakon said, tugging on my sleeve. "Let's look. If we find it, Asa can sleep in it."

I didn't like the spooky shadows in the cargo hold. I didn't like being so far down below. I didn't like hearing that throbbing noise from the other end of the passageway. I began backing up to the door.

"There isn't room in our cabin for the cradle," I reminded Haakon.

He pouted. "Yes, there is. I want to look."

"No, we can't look for the cradle," I told my stubborn brother. "We have to go back up above. They will wonder where we are. It will be time to eat soon. Mama counts on me to look after you, and I say it's time to go."

Haakon kicked one toe against a wooden trunk, but I could see he would do as I said.

"Come on," I said with a sigh of relief. I opened the door to the passageway again. We could see the mist and the red glow at the far end. The throbbing noise was loud in our ears. There was another sharp clank that made us all jump.

"I don't like that door," Hanne said as we tiptoed toward the stairs.

"It's n-n-nothing to be afraid of," I stammered. I could hear Haakon and Hanne both breathing close to my ear.

We tiptoed slower and slower until at last we stopped. We stared at the door like mice staring at a cat. I began to wonder how fast I could run—if I could run.

"Go see what's behind there," Haakon said. He shoved me forward.

I let out a yelp. "NO!" My voice echoed. "No-no-no!"

We all held our breaths.

Then, a terrible growling voice called out from beyond the door. It was a language we could not understand. Suddenly,

the door swung open and crashed against
the wall. There, standing in the doorway in
the mist, was a dark, hairy creature with a
shovel in its hand!

"Troll!" Haakon yelled.

And we turned and ran screaming up
the stairs.

CHAPTER 8

Hide-and-Seek

For three days we didn't dare go lower than the top two decks. When we spoke of the troll in the bottom of the ship, we whispered. And of course, we did not mention him to our parents.

"Do you think he got a good look at us?" Hanne asked.

We were taking turns spitting over the side of the ship. Sailors were working on the top deck at the front of the ship. We could hear them calling to each other.

"I'm not sure," I told Hanne. "I don't think so."

"Do you think he'll try to find us?" Haakon wondered.

The bright sun was making me squint. It had become very hot that afternoon. We left the railing and sat in the shade under a lifeboat. The lifeboats were hung upside down over the deck, which made them a good hiding place for us.

"I can't sleep," Hanne said. "I lie in bed and wonder if he is coming."

"I can't sleep, either," I said.

"I can't sleep because Asa cries at night," Haakon grumbled. "If she had her cradle—"

"Stop talking about the cradle!"

Haakon and Hanne both looked at me in surprise.

"Why are you shouting?" Haakon asked.

"Because"—I pretended that my boot-laces needed to be retied—"we are not going to look for the cradle," I said in a low voice.

Haakon folded his arms and looked cross.

"Come on," I said, crawling out from under the lifeboat. "Let's play a game. Hide-and-seek. I will seek first."

I covered my eyes and began to count out loud. I knew that if I could keep Haakon from thinking of Asa's cradle, he would not suggest we go back down to the cargo hold.

When I had counted to one hundred, I opened my eyes. I looked around me. Life preservers hung on hooks, and coils of rope were stacked on the decks. People strolled arm in arm, and the sailors continued to shout and laugh. I peeked under a lifeboat. Nothing.

"Come out, come out, wherever you are!" I shouted. I ran to the next lifeboat and crawled under it to look. I heard a giggle.

"You found me," Hanne said, popping out from underneath a canvas tarp.

Hanne brushed off her dress and sighed. "You are so lucky to have a brother to play with. And when Asa is bigger, you will have her for a playmate, too. I will have no one when we leave the ship."

I held her hand. We were still in the shade under the lifeboat. "Perhaps we will move to the same town in Minnesota," I told her. "Then we could play together."

"Do you think so?" Hanne asked.

She looked so sad and sorry that I had

to cheer her up. I told her a riddle, and then another, and then I taught her a clapping game. We sat beneath the lifeboat and talked for a very long time. Our stomachs were growling with hunger when we heard Hanne's grandpa calling.

"Hanne? Hanne, where are you?"

Hanne clapped both hands over her mouth. "We will miss dinner!"

I clapped both hands over my mouth, too. "I forgot Haakon!"

Hanne was busy crawling out from our hiding place. "Here I am, Grandpa!" I heard her say, and she was gone.

I sat where I was for a moment, wishing the sick feeling in my stomach would go away. I was supposed to keep an eye on Haakon.

But it looked as if I had lost him again.

As fast as I could, I searched every single hiding place on the top two decks. I looked under each lifeboat, under the chairs and tables, inside the giant coils of rope, everywhere I could think of. Haakon had vanished.

And then I knew that Haakon wasn't on the top two decks.

He had gone searching for Asa's cradle. He had gone down below.

CHAPTER 9

Lili the Scared

I stood at the top of the staircase and looked down into the misty dimness. I could feel my heart knocking against my ribs, as if it wanted to get out and run away. The low, throbbing sound was still coming from below, and the air was warm and damp.

Stubborn Haakon had gone hunting for the cradle. And now I must go hunting for Haakon. I could not return to my parents without my brother. I had to go down—down, down, down below. How I wished I was still Lili the Brave!

I closed my eyes and reached for the banister. I took one step down. I took another step down. I took another and another. The throbbing grew louder, and the air became warmer, but I did not stop. When I reached the bottom step, I counted to three and then opened my eyes.

There was no one in sight. The door on the right was outlined with an orange glow, and steam puffed out around the edge. I held my breath and tiptoed as fast as I could in the opposite direction. I thought the troll would hear my heartbeats, they were so loud! I thought at any moment I would hear a terrible roar behind me.

At last I reached the door of the cargo hold and slipped inside.

"Haakon!" I whispered as loud as I dared.

I listened. Nothing.

"Haakon!" I called again, a little louder.

Then I heard something. Was it a little whimper? A soft sniffle? I crept among the stacks of furniture and trunks, farther and farther, following the sound.

At last I peeked behind a wardrobe. There, squeezed into the Viking-ship cradle, was Haakon. His eyes were shut tight, and his hands were over his ears.

"Haakon!" I said, gently rocking the cradle.

He opened one eye.

"It's me, Lili," I said.

He opened the other eye.

"I was so scared!" Haakon cried. He struggled to get out of the cradle. "I heard the troll coming, so I hid!"

"Well, I have found you now." I took his hand. "Let's go."

We started for the door, but Haakon paused. "The cradle!"

"Haakon!"

"We *have* to take it!"

I shook my head. "Little brothers," I muttered. But I picked up one end of the cradle. "You must help me. I can't carry it alone."

Haakon grabbed the sea monster's head, and we dragged the cradle across the floor. I opened the door and looked out into the passageway. All was clear.

"We must be very quiet," I whispered, putting one finger to my lips.

Haakon nodded. His eyes were as wide and round as a seal's.

We started down the passageway, nervously watching the door at the end. I counted the steps to the staircase as we dragged our Viking ship.

"Just a few more steps," I whispered.

And then the terrible door opened and the terrible voice roared at us in his terrible troll language. Haakon screamed and hid behind me. The troll was covered in soot, and his bristly beard was shiny with sweat. Very slowly, he walked toward us: one step, then another, then another.

Then he darted in front of the stairs. There was no escape!

CHAPTER 10

The Troll

"Stand back!" I shouted. "Don't come any nearer!"

The troll stopped and opened his eyes wide. "Oh, you are a brave little Viking," he said in Norwegian.

"My mama and papa count on me to protect my brother from trolls!" I shouted again. I could feel Haakon shivering and shaking behind me. "Let us by!"

The troll stared at me, and then he began to laugh. He threw his head back and roared with laughter, and he slapped

his knee. A cloud of black dust rose from
his pants.

"Oh, I can tell when I've been beaten!"
he said with a chuckle.

As he laughed, I noticed that he wore

leather boots, as the sailors did. And that although he was very sooty, he wore a uniform, as the sailors did. Haakon poked his head around me to look at the troll.

I folded my arms. "You're not a troll, are you?"

"No, I am not," the man agreed. "My name is Charlie. I'm an American sailor."

"If you're not a troll, then what's all that mist?" Haakon asked in a shaky voice. "And that rumbling sound?"

"I'll show you," Charlie said. He led the way back to his door.

We left the cradle and followed him. The mist grew mistier and the noise grew noisier with each step. I felt very foolish for thinking that Nifelheim was really on a steamship. But I didn't know where Charlie was taking us. The sound was much louder as we went through the door.

We entered a hot, steamy room full of machinery.

"This is the boiler room!" Charlie shouted above the noise. "See, this is the furnace where we burn the coal to boil water. That makes the steam that turns the machinery to make the boat go through the sea! The noise you hear is the machinery!"

And then he picked up his shovel and threw a scoop of black coal onto the roaring flames. Sparks crackled. Then he slammed the iron door on the furnace with a loud *clank!* From pipes over our heads, little bursts of steam went *psst!*

"You see?" Charlie said with a wide smile.

Haakon stared at everything with great

curiosity. "Can you show me how it works?" he asked.

"Tomorrow," Charlie said as he stole a look at a big clock on the wall. "But now it is time for the fireworks."

"Fireworks?" I asked.

"Sure." His smile got even wider. "It's the Fourth of July, a big American holiday. Didn't you know that?"

"No," I said. "We're Norwegian."

Charlie laughed again. "Of course you are. You are brave Viking heroes. And soon you will be Americans, too."

And with that, Charlie shooed us through the boiler room door and along the passageway, and then shooed us up the stairs.

"I will bring your beautiful cradle," Charlie said.

He laughed and joked and teased and growled like a troll, and we thought he was the best troll we'd ever met.

Passengers were hurrying to the top deck. Haakon and I wriggled and squirmed our way through the crowd until we found Mama and Papa and Asa.

"Lili! Haakon! Where have you been?" Mama asked. The sun setting behind her head made her look very beautiful.

"We went to Nifelheim and had an adventure," I said.

"And Lili the Brave rescued me," Haakon said.

There was a loud *CRACK!* And we all looked up. A flash of red and yellow stars burst over the water. The ship's brass band began to play a marching tune. Another burst of fireworks turned the sky green and white and pink. Then purple and gold. Then red, white, and blue.

"It is like the northern lights," Papa said. "Just as beautiful."

I put my hand in Papa's. "I think I will like it in America," I told him. "I'm not afraid to go."

A Little Bit of History

The Vikings—also called Norsemen—were the sea-faring warriors of Scandinavia (Norway, Sweden, and Denmark). They were the world's best ship-builders, and often put large carvings of mythical animals on the fronts of their ships to terrify their enemies. From the 800s to the early 1000s, they sailed up and down the coast of Europe, attacking and plundering and taking captives. They were fierce people, and had many myths and legends related to battle, bravery, and exploration. One of the most important Norse gods was Thor the Thunderer, the fiercest Viking of all.

Because Scandinavia is rugged and cold, the Vikings were always in search of new places to set-tle and build towns. Historians now know that the Vikings were actually the first to sail to North America, centuries before Christopher Columbus. There were Viking settlements in Greenland and along the coast of northern Canada. Some histori-ans believe the Norsemen even sailed as far south as New England.

When monks brought Christianity to Scandi-

71

navia, the Vikings stopped making war, but they kept their legends and their knowledge of ships and handed them down from generation to generation. Norway, Sweden, and Denmark were still rugged and cold, and by the 1800s they were also extremely crowded. There was very little land for farming, so it was hard to make a living. Many people also wished to live in a democracy: they were tired of living with kings and princes who got to make all the rules. The descendants of the Vikings were still hoping for new places to live.

By 1869, railroads in America stretched from coast to coast. The railroad companies needed settlers to build new towns along their lines. Many of these companies sent people like Mr. Rolvang to Europe to invite immigrants to move to America. Thousands of Scandinavians like the Alesund family sailed across the ocean and took the train to the state of Minnesota. Today you can find many people in Minnesota with Norwegian, Swedish, and Danish names like Andersen, Holmquist, and Larsen.

The wind blows strong and steady on the Minnesota prairie. Sometimes when it ripples over the wheat fields, a big cloud on the horizon looks like a Viking ship sailing over the ocean to adventure.

Glossary

cloudberries Small pink berries, like raspberries, that grow in Norway

fjord (f'yord) A narrow, deep sea inlet, usually with a very steep shoreline

glacier (glay-sher) A huge mass of ice; in northern countries, a glacier never melts completely

speaking tube A tube that carries the sound of a voice from one place to another

hostel A kind of hotel

rommegrøt (room-a-groot) A creamy porridge made with milk and butter

About the Author

JENNIFER ARMSTRONG traveled to Norway when she was twelve. "I'll never forget seeing the northern lights in the sky, and the jellyfish in the fjords. And since the sun didn't set until ten o'clock, I could stay up late reading every night."

Jennifer Armstrong has been reading and writing since she was in first grade. That was when she decided to become an author. She has written many picture books and historical novels for children, including *Black-Eyed Susan*. She lives in Saratoga Springs, New York, in a very old house that might—just might—have a troll in the basement.